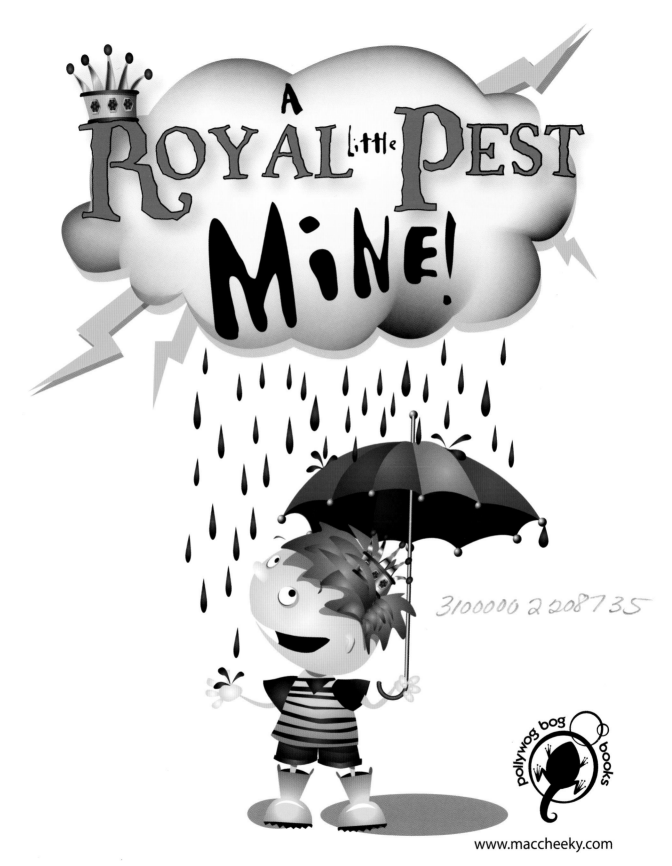

A ROYAL little PEST
Mine!

3100000 2208735

pollywog bog books

www.maccheeky.com

BY ANITA REYNOLDS MACARTHUR & ILLUSTRATED BY KAREN ROY

The illustrations in this book were created digitally using Adobe Illustrator CS4.
The type is set in 14 point Gill Sans, Whiffy, and Naughties.

Library and Archives Canada Cataloguing in Publication

Reynolds MacArthur, Anita, 1968-
A royal little pest: mine! / by Anita Reynolds MacArthur ; & illustrated
by Karen Roy.

(MacCheeky series ; 2nd)
ISBN 978-0-9810575-1-4

I. Roy, Karen, 1962- II. Title.
III. Series: Reynolds MacArthur, Anita, 1968-. MacCheeky series.

PS8635.E96R693 2010   jC813'.6   C2009-902223-0

Distributed by Fitzhenry & Whiteside Limited

10 9 8 7 6 5 4 3 2

Printed in Hong Kong, China, by Paramount Printing Company in January 2011, Job 131001

To Mum and Poppies. Thanks for teaching me to trust my instincts and to follow my dreams. — A.R.M.

To Robert, Jocelynn, Mac, Shirley, and my sisters, Sue and Cheryl. It wouldn't be nearly as much fun without you. Thank you for your love. — K.R.

A big thank you to Dianne Reynolds and Liz Arnsby for going beyond the beyond.

And, once again, a heartfelt thank you to Adele Reynolds and Susan McFayden.

4

Prince Hayden MacCheeky was a REAL little prince. He lived in a royal castle on a royal lane with his royal parents, his royal brother Prince Campbell, his royal sister Princess Ava, and his royal dog Goober.

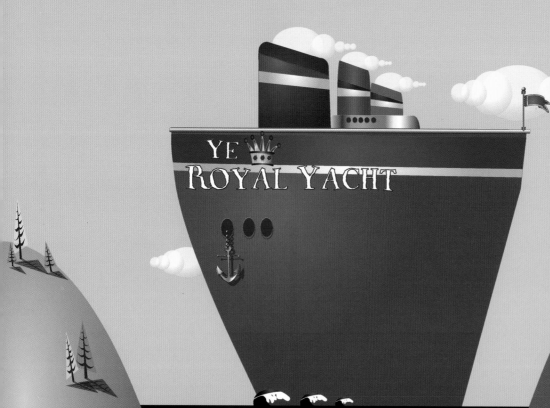

Prince Hayden MacCheeky was a mover and a shaker. He was ALWAYS busy doing something.

From the moment he woke up, until the moment he went to bed, Prince Hayden MacCheeky NEVER stopped moving, not even for a minute!

Prince Hayden LOVED playing on his own with HIS royal toys.

Each morning, Prince Hayden played in his royal bedroom stacking HIS royal blocks and then knocking them down.

HONK! HONK! CRASH!

Each afternoon, Prince Hayden played in the royal hallway crashing HIS royal trucks into one another.

And each evening, Prince Hayden played in the royal backyard bouncing HIS royal bouncy ball.

BOING!

Prince Hayden had SO much fun playing on his own with HIS royal toys that he NEVER wanted to share them with anyone else.

One morning, Prince Hayden saw Princess Ava playing with HIS royal blocks.

"MINE!" yelled Prince Hayden, his face turning red.
He GRABBED the royal blocks and THREW them across the room!

Prince Hayden's not sharing!

"No yelling! No throwing!" said Princess Ava crossly.

"Prince Hayden's not sharing!" shouted Princess Ava to ANYONE within earshot as she turned and stomped away.

That afternoon, Prince Hayden saw Prince Campbell playing with HIS royal trucks.

"MINE!" screeched Prince Hayden, his face turning redder. He GRABBED the royal trucks and THREW them across the room!

"No screeching! No throwing!" said Prince Campbell crossly.

"Prince Hayden's not sharing!" shouted Prince Campbell to ANYONE within earshot as he turned and stomped away.

And that evening, Prince Hayden saw his royal dog Goober playing with HIS royal bouncy ball.

"MINE! ALL MINE!" yelled and screeched Prince Hayden, his face turning EVEN redder. He GRABBED the royal bouncy ball and THREW it across the yard!

"WOOF! WOOF! WOOF!" barked Goober crossly.

"WOOF!" barked Goober to ANYONE within earshot
as she turned and stomped away.

The next day, the king made a royal announcement.

"We are going to visit your royal cousin Princess Ella," he announced to the royal MacCheeky siblings.

Princess Ella had some of the FINEST royal toys in the land!

"Yay! Princess Ella!" squealed the royal MacCheeky siblings excitedly as they raced out the royal front door of the royal castle.

19

When they arrived at
Princess Ella's royal castle,
Prince Hayden raced...

THROUGH the royal front door,

PAST the royal dining room,

and INTO the royal toy room.

Prince Hayden was SO excited to be in Princess Ella's royal toy room that he didn't notice her big grumpy FROWN.

Prince Hayden scooped up one of Princess Ella's royal
teddy bears into his arms.

"MINE!" yelled Princess Ella, her face turning red.
She GRABBED the royal teddy bear and THREW it across the room!

Prince Hayden was SHOCKED by Princess Ella's outburst.
She hurt his feelings.

Then, Prince Hayden picked up one of Princess Ella's royal books.
"MINE!" screeched Princess Ella, her face turning redder.

24

She GRABBED the royal book and THREW it across the room!

Prince Hayden was STUNNED by Princess Ella's outburst.
She hurt his feelings AGAIN.

Finally, Prince Hayden picked up one of Princess Ella's royal puzzles.

"MINE! ALL MINE!" yelled and screeched Princess Ella, her face turning EVEN redder!

She GRABBED the royal puzzle and THREW it across the room!

Prince Hayden was shocked AND stunned by Princess Ella's outburst.

She hurt his feelings YET AGAIN!

Prince Hayden couldn't touch ANYTHING without
Princess Ella yelling or screeching at him.

This wasn't fun at all. It REALLY hurt his feelings.

"No yelling! No screeching! No throwing!"
shouted Prince Hayden crossly.

"You're not sharing and that's not fun!"
he blurted out.

Prince Hayden looked puzzled and wondered...

Did I really say that?

He strolled out the back door and into Princess Ella's royal garden.

beets

carrots

beets

30

Sharing didn't hurt other people's feelings, and it made HIM feel good too.

Prince Hayden realized that a little royal sharing leads to a lot of royal fun for EVERYONE.

carrots

One, Two & You
Little Yellow
Leonard Lightbulb
Dancing Sarah

cookie time box

From that day forward, Prince Hayden MacCheeky decided to SHARE his royal toys instead of keeping them all to himself.

And he NEVER yelled, screeched, or threw his royal toys EVER again.

The end